The Growing Story

By Ruth Krauss

Illustrated by Helen Oxenbury

HarperCollins *Children's Books*

First published in hardback in Great Britain
by HarperCollins Children's Books in 2007

1 3 5 7 9 10 8 6 4 2
ISBN-13: 978-0-00-723332-8
ISBN-10: 0-00-723332-9

Text copyright © Ruth Krauss 1947, 1975
Illustrations copyright © Helen Oxenbury 2007

HarperCollins Children's Books is a division of HarperCollins Publishers Ltd.

Visit our website at: www.harpercollinschildrensbooks.co.uk

Printed and bound in China

For Tom
H.O.

A boy and a puppy and some
chicks were all very little.

Summer was coming.
Buds grew on the trees. The grass
began to grow. On the side of the
barn, flowers began to grow.
The little boy said to his mother,
'Everything is growing. The grass
is growing. The flowers are
growing. The trees are growing.'

He asked her,
'Will the chicks grow?'
'Of course,' his mother replied.

He asked her,
'Will the puppy grow?'
'Of course,' his mother replied.
He asked her, 'Will I grow too?'
'Of course you'll grow too,'
his mother replied.

The days grew longer.

The nights grew shorter.

The grass grew faster. The flowers grew higher.

Leaves grew big on the trees.

The little boy said to the puppy and the chicks,
'We're growing too.'

The air was growing warmer.
The little boy and his mother
planted corn seeds in the field.
His mother said, 'We'll put away your warm
woollen clothes. When summer is over
you'll put them on again.'

They folded up his warm trousers
and put them away in a box.
They folded up his warm coat
and put it away in the box.

The little boy climbed on a chair and
put the box on a shelf.

The corn grew. Blossoms grew on the orchard trees.

Lilacs bloomed by the barn.

The chicks grew taller. The puppy grew taller.

The little boy said, 'You both grew taller.'

He said to his mother,
'They both grew taller. I don't feel taller.'
He asked her, 'Am I growing too?'
'Oh yes. Of course,' his mother replied.

Little pears grew on the orchard trees.

Little ears grew on the corn.

The grass grew still faster.

The chicks grew still taller.

The puppy grew still taller.

The little boy looked in a mirror.

He said to his mother, 'The chicks have grown taller than my knee.

The puppy has grown taller than my middle. I don't look taller.'

He asked her, 'Are you sure I am growing?'

His mother replied, 'Of course you are growing.'

The honeysuckle bloomed.

The roses bloomed.

The corn grew as high as a man.

The pears were ripening.

The chicks grew still taller again.

The puppy grew still taller again.

The little boy went alone and sat by the side of the barn.

He looked at the grass and the flowers.

He looked at the trees and the corn.

He looked at the puppy and looked at the chicks.

He said, 'Everything is still growing. I can see they are growing.' He asked, 'Can I really be growing too?'

When the leaves grew red and yellow and brown,
summer was over. The corn was over. No flowers
bloomed on the side of the barn.
The chicks had grown up. The chicks were chickens.
The chickens were nearly up to the little boy's middle.

The puppy had grown up. The puppy was a dog.

The dog was nearly up to the little boy's head.

The little boy looked at the chickens and the dog.

'You both have grown up. I haven't grown up.

I am still little,' the little boy said.

The air had grown colder.
The little boy's mother said,
'We'll take out your warm woollen clothes
and put them on again.'
The little boy climbed on the chair
and took down the box from the shelf.
They took out his warm trousers from
the box and unfolded them.
They took out his warm coat from
the box and unfolded it.

The little boy put on his
warm trousers again
and looked in the mirror.
'My trousers are too tight.
The legs are too short,' he said.

He put on the warm coat again
and looked in the mirror.
'My coat is too tight.
The sleeves are too short,' he said.

'I'm
growing
too.'